W9-AJM-230

A NOTE TO PARENTS

When your children are ready to "step into reading," giving them the right books is as crucial as giving them the right food to eat. **Step into Reading Books** present exciting stories and information reinforced with lively, colorful illustrations that make learning to read fun, satisfying, and worthwhile. They are priced so that acquiring an entire library of them is affordable. And they are beginning readers with a difference—they're written on five levels.

Early Step into Reading Books are designed for brand-new readers, with large type and only one or two lines of very simple text per page. **Step 1 Books** feature the same easy-to-read type as the Early Step into Reading Books, but with more words per page. **Step 2 Books** are both longer and slightly more difficult, while **Step 3 Books** introduce readers to paragraphs and fully developed plot lines. **Step 4 Books** offer exciting nonfiction for the increasingly independent reader.

The grade levels assigned to the five steps—preschool through kindergarten for the Early Books, preschool through grade 1 for Step 1, grades 1 through 3 for Step 2, grades 2 through 3 for Step 3, and grades 2 through 4 for Step 4—are intended only as guides. Some children move through all five steps very rapidly; others climb the steps over a period of several years. Either way, these books will help your child "step into reading" in style!

http://www.randomhouse.com/
http://www.sesamestreet.com

Library of Congress Cataloging-in-Publication Data
Albee, Sarah. I can do it! : featuring Jim Henson's Sesame Street Muppets / by Sarah Albee ; illustrated by Larry DiFiori. p. cm. — (Step into reading. Step 1 book)
SUMMARY: Zoe and her friends at Sesame Street can do all sorts of things, especially when they help each other.
ISBN: 0-679-88687-7 (pbk.) — ISBN: 0-679-98687-1 (lib. bdg.)
[1. Helpfulness—Fiction. 2. Stories in rhyme.] I. DiFiori, Lawrence, ill.
II. Title. III. Series. PZ7.A3174Iae 1997 [E]—dc21 96-53135

Printed in the United States of America 10 9 8 7 6 5 4 3 2 1

STEP INTO READING is a registered trademark of Random House, Inc.

Step into Reading®

I Can Do It!

**Featuring
Jim Henson's
Sesame Street
Muppets**

By Sarah Albee
Illustrated by Larry DiFiori

A Step 1 Book

Random House ⌂ New York
Children's Television Workshop

I can write my name.

I can draw a smile.

We can rake the leaves,
then jump into the pile.

I can slide down a slide.

I can make a cat from clay.

I can eat a lima bean.

I can dance ballet.

I don't know how
to tie my shoe.
With the help of a friend
I can learn that, too!

I can bang on a drum.

I can reach a high shelf.

I can comb my fur.

I can pour my juice myself.

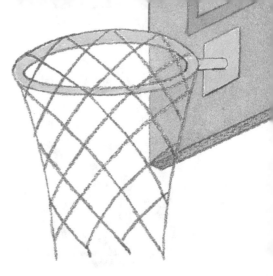

I'm too small
to dunk the ball.

I need help from my friend who is eight feet tall.

I can button my shirt.

I can string some beads.

We can jump so high.

We can plant some seeds.

I'm too little
for a two-wheel bike.
My friend is too big
to fit on my trike!

25

I can't read this book.

You can't climb this tree.

I can help you up.

You can read to me!

I can carry the cups.

I can carry the plates.

Please do not try this
on roller skates!

I can watch a parade,
but little Natasha can't see!
She needs help from...

...a big monster like me!